THE USBORNE YOUNG SCIENTIST
TELEVISION

Christopher Griffin-Beale and Robyn Gee

Edited by Lynn Inglis

Designed by Nigel Reece, Ruth Russell and Roger Priddy

Illustrated by Guy Smith, Graham Round, Richard Johnson,
Chris Lyon, Ian Stephen, Graham Smith, Philip Schramm and Joe McEwan

Contents

Technical consultant: Charles Osborne

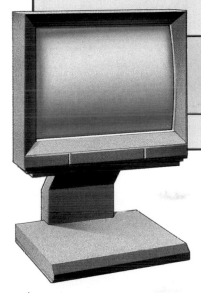

The TV revolution

Sixty years ago it seemed miraculous that pictures and sound could be sent through the air. The TV system that we use today was developed during the 1930s. The 1950s saw the first TV revolution, with TV sets in millions of homes and more companies to broadcast to them.

In the last few years another TV revolution has begun. This revolution is about the choices available to the viewer. It has been brought about by great advances in technology, especially the invention of the microchip. This has allowed the development of sophisticated video equipment, but cheap and easy enough to use at home. Now you can use your television to watch programmes bounced from satellites in space, to receive instantly updated information, see new movies on video and even to watch videos you have made yourself.

TV companies make and transmit TV programmes or buy them from other companies.

This big aerial broadcasts the TV signal.

You can use the TV to shop from home, phoning to order what you see on the screen in some programmes. Others have phone-in voting for viewers, about issues or talent spots.

Stereo speaker

Subtitles

Some TV broadcasts and videos are made in stereo sound and a TV with stereo speakers, like this, will be able to pick it up. Stereo TV sounds even better if played through a hi-fi system's speakers instead of the television's small ones.

Many stations broadcast screens of text and picture information, called teletext. Text can also be combined with ordinary programmes. For example, subtitles that display the words spoken on a programme, for people who cannot hear well, are shown here.

Special still video (SV) cameras can be used for snapshots like any ordinary camera. Your pictures are stored inside the camera on a magnetic disk, similar to a computer's floppy disk. You then attach the camera to a video cassette recorder by a lead, display the pictures on the TV screen and record those you want to keep on ordinary video tape. As the disk is erasable, it can be used again many times.

Still video disk

Some video players use a small part of the screen to show what is on a tape or being broadcast on another channel. So, you can keep an eye on one programme at the same time as watching another.

With a video cassette recorder you can record broadcast programmes to watch later and play pre-recorded video tapes you have bought, rented or even made yourself.

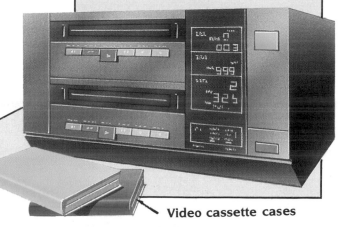

Video cassette cases

A home video camera like this records scenes on to video tape, for you to play back later on your video cassette recorder.

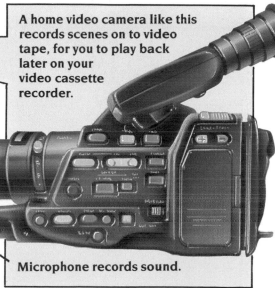

Microphone records sound.

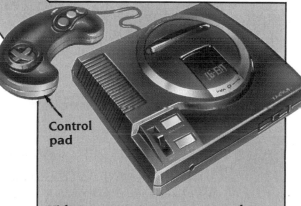

Control pad

Video or computer games consoles can play various games tapes. The console plugs into your TV set, which acts as a screen for the game.

Useful TV

As well as providing hours of entertainment, TV and video technology is being put to work in many different and useful areas.

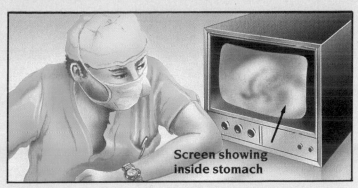

Screen showing inside stomach

Video cameras are used by surgeons for some operations, and help to save having to cut the patient open. To operate on stomach ulcers, for example, the surgeon passes an instrument called an endoscope down into the patient's stomach. This is a thin tube of optical fibres, some of which carry a laser beam to treat the ulcer. Others carry back an image of the inside of the stomach.

The resulting picture is shown on a TV screen, so the doctors can see what they are doing, as they operate on the ulcers.

Monitors show different parts of a building.

Security video cameras keep watch in car parks, shopping centres and other public places. Some, like those in banks, make a tape of what they "see", in case there is a crime. Others send a live picture to be monitored by the security company, as shown above.

Camera recording traffic flow.

Video cameras are also used to help traffic control. They send pictures of traffic building up at busy junctions to traffic control offices. The staff are able to program the traffic lights to help the traffic flow smoothly without jams.

Broadcasting

TV broadcasting is the process of sending out pictures and sound through the air. It developed from two other important inventions: cinema photography (a way of capturing and reproducing moving images on film) and radio broadcasting (sending sound through the air on radio waves).

Once people had discovered how to capture pictures electronically and to make radio waves carry moving images as well as sound, television had been invented. The word "tele-vision" means "seeing at a distance".

All the broadcast pictures that you see on your TV screen are either "live", which means that the action is happening as you see it, or "prerecorded", that is recorded before being broadcast.

Prerecorded pictures are recorded either on film by a cine camera, or on video tape by a video camera, or TV studio camera and video tape recorder. Some programmes are made up of a mixture of live and prerecorded material.

Live programmes

In the early days of TV all programmes were broadcast live. Now most are recorded before being broadcast. Those that still go out live are the ones where it is important to use the latest information, such as the news.

Even live programmes are usually recorded during transmission so that there is a copy to refer to or to show again.

Live news broadcast

TV camera

Prerecording on video tape

Video tape recording has been used in television since the late 1950s. The images and sounds are sent by the TV cameras and microphones to a video recorder, which records them on magnetic tape like that used in home video cassettes. Prerecorded tapes are stored in a video library ready to be played back when it is time to broadcast them. Mistakes can be cut out and new bits put in before broadcast.

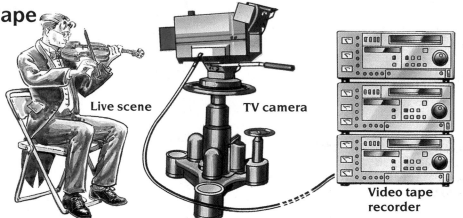
Live scene

TV camera

Video tape recorder

Prerecording on film

Some programmes are recorded on film, where the picture is recorded on a plastic tape, coated with light sensitive chemical. Like ordinary photographs, cine film must be developed after it has been shot. Before it can be broadcast, material recorded on film has to be run through a "telecine" machine, which converts the film images into electronic TV signals. They are then transmitted in the same way as other TV signals.

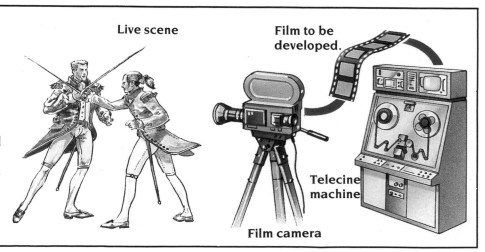
Live scene

Film to be developed.

Telecine machine

Film camera

Stages in a TV broadcast

This page shows the different stages that a TV picture goes through before you see it. The four main stages are: Production – planning and making television programmes; Transmission – sending the programme out; Reception – picking up the signal and Display – showing the picture on the TV screen.

This live scene is taking place in a TV studio.

The production stage is carried out by television companies working in TV stations.

The microphone converts sound from the scene into electronic messages and sends them down a cable to the control room.

The TV camera converts light from the live scene into electronic signals and sends the signals down the cable to the control room.

In the control room, pictures from various sources are selected and checked before being sent out of the transmitting station.

The video tape machine sends electronic signals from the video tape along cables to the control room.

The telecine machine converts pictures and sound from films into electronic signals and sends them down a cable to the control room.

A TV aerial or satellite dish picks up the electronic signals carried by radio waves. These then travel down a cable to the TV set.

Radio signals can also be broadcast into space by dish aerials. They bounce off a satellite and are picked up by home satellite dish aerials.

In the transmitting station the transmitter combines the sound and picture signals with radio waves.

The radio waves carrying the sound and picture signals are sent out into the air in all directions from the top of a transmitting mast.

TV sets convert the electronic signals back into sound and pictures.

Underground cables can also carry the TV signals into homes.

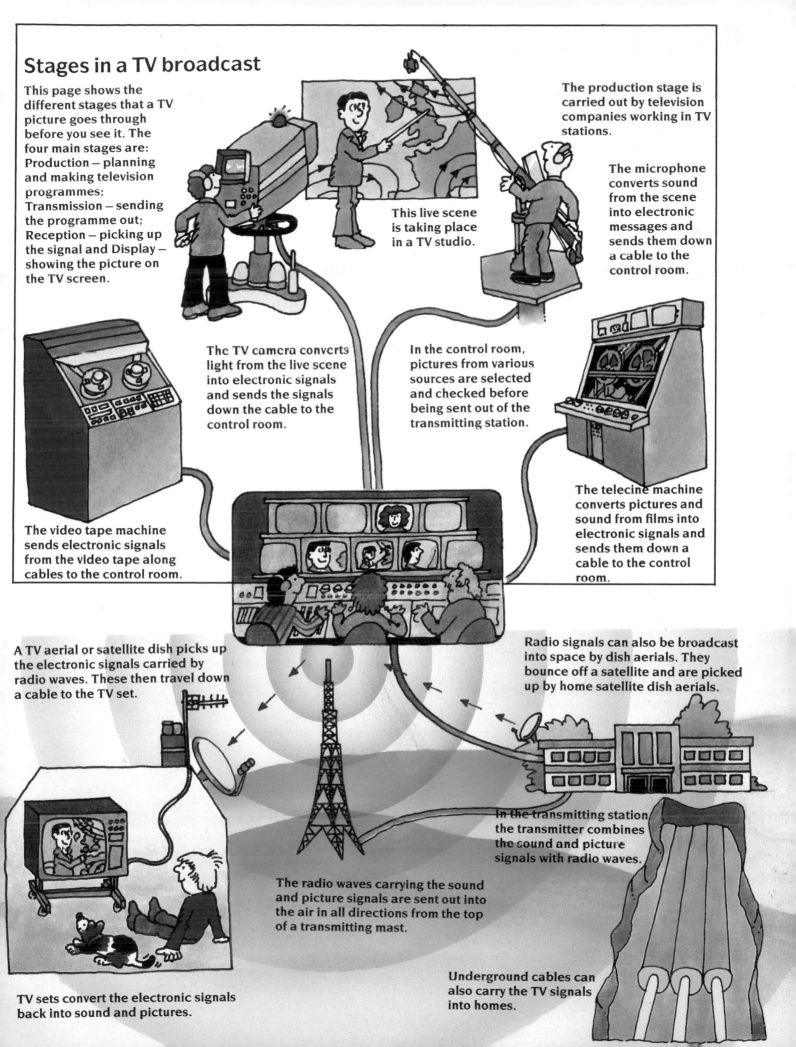

TV and video cameras

TV and video cameras work by turning light into electric currents. There is no film or video tape inside a studio camera. The electric currents, or picture signals, are sent down a cable and either broadcast straight away ("live") or sent to a video tape recorder to be stored and transmitted later. Live programmes are usually also recorded at the same time as they are broadcast.

Video cameras work in the same way as TV cameras, but are smaller and lighter. However, there is a video tape inside the camera, which records the picture and sounds as they are taken.

Studio TV camera

There are several different kinds of TV camera. This picture shows the type used in many TV studios. They all work in the same way, but smaller, portable cameras are used for different jobs such as news gathering or outside broadcasts (see pages 12-13) where conditions are different from the studio.

This steering ring is used by the camera operator to steer the camera around the studio and to turn it towards the action. The camera can also be raised and lowered and swung from side to side.

This is the cable that carries the electronic picture signals out of the camera to the control room (see pages 14-15). It also brings in the electricity to power the camera and instructions (known as "talkback") from the director which the operator hears over headphones.

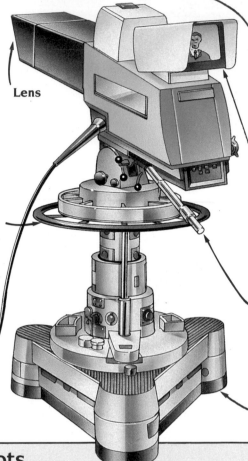

Lens

This red light goes on when the camera is being used to record or transmit. It lets the people being "shot" know which camera to look at and helps the production staff keep track of which camera is being used.

This is the viewfinder. It is a miniature TV screen and shows the camera operator exactly the picture that the camera is recording or broadcasting. If the camera is waiting to be used in a live programme, the viewfinder can show the picture that is being transmitted. This helps the operator to follow what is going on.

This handle controls the zoom lens (see below) and there is a knob on the opposite side to focus the lens.

Studio cameras are often mounted on wheeled stands called dollies, so that they can be moved around smoothly without camera shake.

Camera lenses and shots

Most cameras have a zoom lens as it gives a range of different picture sizes while the camera stays in a fixed position. A zoom lens can alter the picture from a long-shot to a close-up very smoothly and quickly. Other types of lenses are used for special shots.

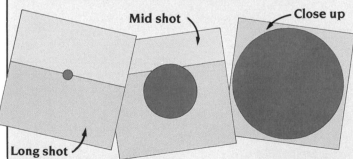

Mid shot

Close up

Long shot

A macro lens is used for very close-up pictures, when the camera is extremely near to the subject. They can be used to film tiny insects, for example, making them fill the screen, as here.

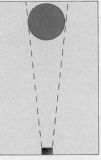
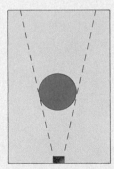
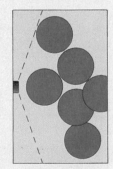

Narrow angle   Normal angle   Wide angle

A narrow angle lens produces close-up shots of very distant subjects, without too much distracting background. For instance at a racetrack, the camera might be in a fixed position a long way from the action.

A wide angle lens is used when the camera is close to the scene but needs to get a wide view, in a room, for example. The camera cannot get far enough away to capture the whole scene with a normal lens, but the wide angle lens takes in the whole view.

How TV and video cameras work

Cameras work rather like eyes. You see things because light reflected from them enters your eye. It is turned into signals which your brain decodes and sees as a picture. To turn a live scene into a picture on a TV screen, a TV camera has to convert the entire scene into a series of electric messages. It does this by turning light from the scene into electricity. The TV set turns the electricity back into pictures.

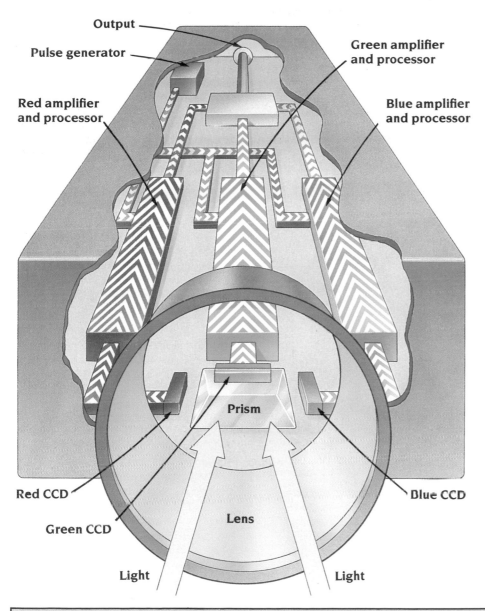

Output

Pulse generator

Green amplifier and processor

Red amplifier and processor

Blue amplifier and processor

Prism

Red CCD

Blue CCD

Green CCD

Lens

Light

Light

In a TV camera, light passes through the lens into a prism. This prism has special filters that split the light into its red, blue and green elements. Red, blue and green are the three primary colours that mix to make any other colour out of light. Each stream of coloured light then falls on to a kind of microchip called a charged coupled device, or CCD for short, which turns it into electricity.

There are three CCDs, one for each colour, so there are separate electrical signals for the red, the blue and the green. The signals are all strengthened and processed by another chip. This processing ensures that the signals are balanced and that the picture will be sharp and free from interference.
Another chip called the pulse generator controls the rate at which the three CCDs and processors work.

The signals are then combined in a coder which produces the output which can be turned back into a picture by a TV. There are several different ways of coding the signal. Most of Western Europe uses a system called PAL. France has a system known as SECAM and the American system is NTSC. Other parts of the world have adopted one of these. The systems are not compatible and you must have the right kind of TV set for the signals.

How a CCD works

A CCD is coated with a light sensitive chemical which changes light into electricity. There are many rows of tiny cells, rather like the solar cells used to produce electricity from sunlight.
The cells produce a varying electric signal in response to the amount of light falling on them: strong light produces a strong electric signal, weak light produces a weak signal.

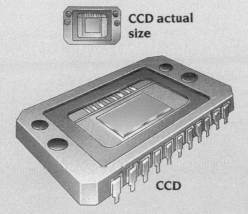

CCD actual size

CCD

Each cell is measured in turn in a process called scanning. This is done in the same way as you read all the words on a page, from left to right, and top to bottom.
In the PAL system there are 625 lines of cells and they are all read 25 times a second. In America and Japan a different television system, known as NTSC, is used which has 525 lines that are read 30 times per second.

Television sound

The sound on a television programme is as important as the picture. Television production companies take as much care to get the right kind and quality of sound as they do with pictures. Like pictures, sound can be broadcast immediately or stored on tape with the picture signals.

In the early 1990s, stereo sound began to be broadcast with some programmes. You need to have a decoder and stereo speakers on your television set in order to be able to hear the stereo effect.

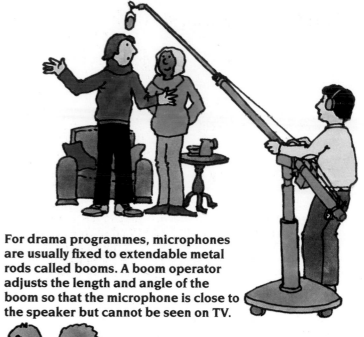

Microphones

The main piece of TV equipment for capturing sound is a microphone. Different kinds of microphone are used in making TV programmes, depending on the situation and the kind of sound. Sometimes many microphones are used for just one programme. Here are some examples.

For drama programmes, microphones are usually fixed to extendable metal rods called booms. A boom operator adjusts the length and angle of the boom so that the microphone is close to the speaker but cannot be seen on TV.

Musicians sometimes use microphones fixed to adjustable metal stands.

A hand-held microphone is often used outside, where several people may need it for only a short time and interviewers want to move around.

Small microphones pinned to clothing are often used on chat shows and by newsreaders.

Radio microphones

All the microphones shown here have wires connecting them to a tape recorder or the sound mixing desk. Radio microphones are small and light and do not have any wires. They are used when a presenter is moving around a lot, for example, walking or driving past the camera.

The presenter carries a small radio transmitter which sends the sound picked up by the microphone to a nearby receiver. A cable then takes the sound to the mixing desk or tape recorder.

Picking up the right sounds

One problem sound engineers have to cope with is how to pick up the sound they want, without picking up sounds that they do not want. They do this by selecting and positioning microphones very carefully and by adjusting the distance from which they will pick up sound. Different microphones have different sensitivities to the sounds around them.

Some microphones pick up sounds equally from all directions. These are called omnidirectional or omnis for short.

A microphone that picks up sound from the front and has a dead area behind it is called a cardioid or directional.

Some microphones pick up sound on either side. These are called bidirectional and are useful for two speakers facing each other.

How a microphone works

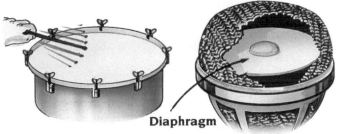

Diaphragm

Moving coil microphone — Diaphragm

Coil of wire — Magnet

All sound is caused by something vibrating. Vibrations travel through the air and make other objects vibrate in response. The sounds you hear are the vibrations of your ear drum.

Inside a microphone is a sensitive, metal plate called a diaphragm. It vibrates in response to sound vibrations. Louder sounds make it move further; higher sounds make it move faster.

Attached to the diaphragm is a device which turns vibrations into electric signals. The devices for doing this give different microphones their names – moving coil, ribbon and capacitor.

Moving coil microphones have a magnet and a thin coil of wire attached to the diaphragm. When a wire moves near a magnet an electric current begins to flow. This current becomes the sound signal.

The sound mixing desk

In a live programme, the electrical signals from the microphones go direct to the sound mixing desk. This machine deals with the input from the many microphones used on a programme. There will often be sounds from many other sources to deal with as well, such as sounds on tape, the opening music, or soundtrack from a film. Other sound sources can be live, such as telephone calls, sound from other studios or outside broadcasts.

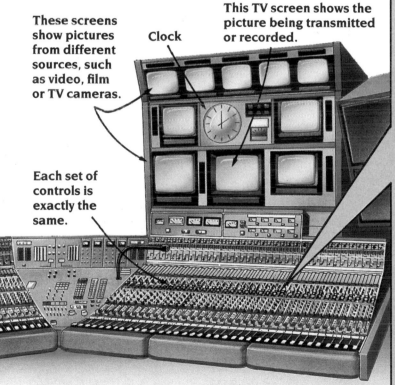

These screens show pictures from different sources, such as video, film or TV cameras.

Clock

This TV screen shows the picture being transmitted or recorded.

Each set of controls is exactly the same.

The sound mixer has to operate the controls for each of the channels, all at once. As many as 40 different sources can be used in a single programme. When a broadcast is live this is all done as the programme is transmitted. With taped programmes the final sound is recorded at the same time as the pictures and they are put on a master video tape together.

The controls

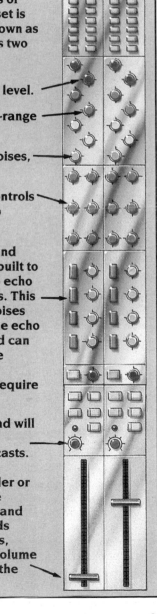

Although the mixing desk looks very complicated it actually consists of many identical controls. Each set is for one sound source and is known as a "channel". This picture shows two sound channels in close up.

Amplification: boosts the sound level.

Equalization: adjusts bass, mid-range and treble sounds.

Filtering: removes unwanted noises, such as the rumble of traffic.

Public address (known as PA): controls the sound relayed to the studio audience.

Echo: is added to make the sound more "hollow". TV studios are built to be acoustically "dead", with no echo or unwanted backgound noises. This means that voices and other noises sound very dull and lifeless. The echo effect gives them more life, and can be adjusted to match the scene created; it may be indoors or outdoors, for example, which require different kinds of sound.

Pan: controls whether the sound will be heard from the left or right loudspeaker for stereo broadcasts.

Volume: makes the sound louder or quieter (known as fading). The operator slides this handle up and down. Each sound source needs individual adjustment as voices, instruments and so on vary in volume and need to be balanced with the other sounds being used.

In a TV studio

Most TV programmes are made inside TV studios. A television station or centre usually contains several studios of different sizes. Attached to each studio is a set of three control rooms: the sound control room, the lighting and vision control room and the production control room. A central control room coordinates all the programmes and links material broadcast by the station.

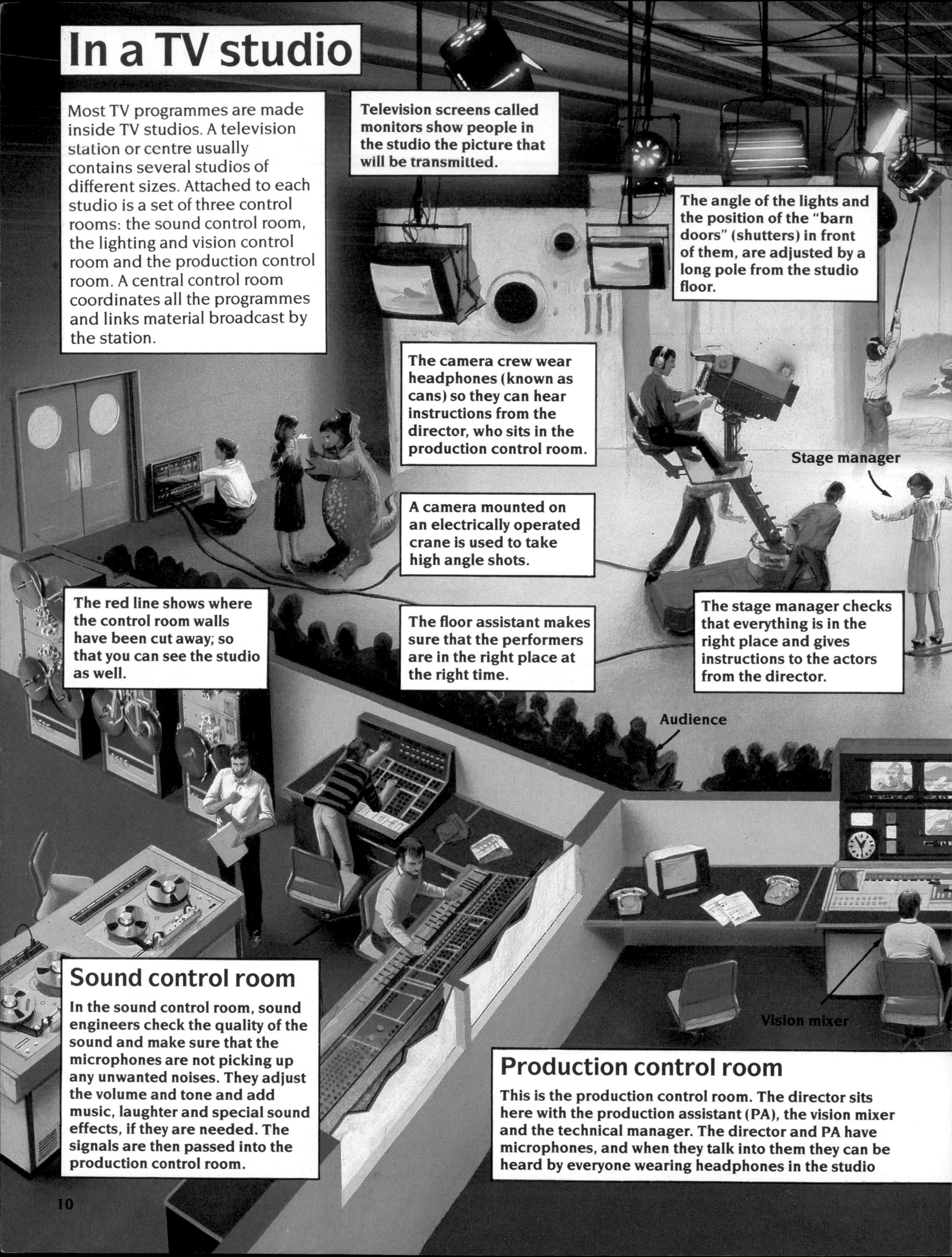

Television screens called monitors show people in the studio the picture that will be transmitted.

The angle of the lights and the position of the "barn doors" (shutters) in front of them, are adjusted by a long pole from the studio floor.

The camera crew wear headphones (known as cans) so they can hear instructions from the director, who sits in the production control room.

Stage manager

A camera mounted on an electrically operated crane is used to take high angle shots.

The red line shows where the control room walls have been cut away; so that you can see the studio as well.

The floor assistant makes sure that the performers are in the right place at the right time.

The stage manager checks that everything is in the right place and gives instructions to the actors from the director.

Audience

Sound control room

In the sound control room, sound engineers check the quality of the sound and make sure that the microphones are not picking up any unwanted noises. They adjust the volume and tone and add music, laughter and special sound effects, if they are needed. The signals are then passed into the production control room.

Vision mixer

Production control room

This is the production control room. The director sits here with the production assistant (PA), the vision mixer and the technical manager. The director and PA have microphones, and when they talk into them they can be heard by everyone wearing headphones in the studio

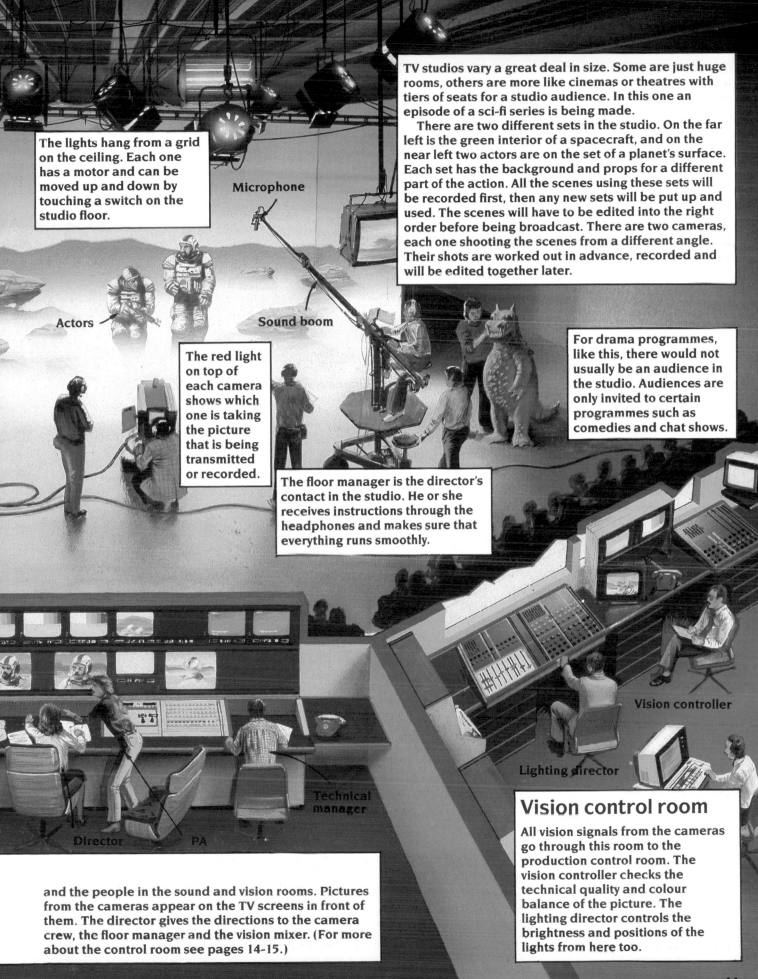

The lights hang from a grid on the ceiling. Each one has a motor and can be moved up and down by touching a switch on the studio floor.

Microphone

TV studios vary a great deal in size. Some are just huge rooms, others are more like cinemas or theatres with tiers of seats for a studio audience. In this one an episode of a sci-fi series is being made.

There are two different sets in the studio. On the far left is the green interior of a spacecraft, and on the near left two actors are on the set of a planet's surface. Each set has the background and props for a different part of the action. All the scenes using these sets will be recorded first, then any new sets will be put up and used. The scenes will have to be edited into the right order before being broadcast. There are two cameras, each one shooting the scenes from a different angle. Their shots are worked out in advance, recorded and will be edited together later.

Actors

Sound boom

The red light on top of each camera shows which one is taking the picture that is being transmitted or recorded.

For drama programmes, like this, there would not usually be an audience in the studio. Audiences are only invited to certain programmes such as comedies and chat shows.

The floor manager is the director's contact in the studio. He or she receives instructions through the headphones and makes sure that everything runs smoothly.

Vision controller

Lighting director

Technical manager

Director   **PA**

Vision control room

All vision signals from the cameras go through this room to the production control room. The vision controller checks the technical quality and colour balance of the picture. The lighting director controls the brightness and positions of the lights from here too.

and the people in the sound and vision rooms. Pictures from the cameras appear on the TV screens in front of them. The director gives the directions to the camera crew, the floor manager and the vision mixer. (For more about the control room see pages 14-15.)

Outside the studios

Programme makers often have to go outside the studios for the material they need. This presents different problems and so different equipment is often used. Events that need several cameras and are to be broadcast live (like this sports meeting) are covered by "outside broadcast units". This means taking along TV cameras and a travelling control room with a team of people.

Until the 1980s, almost all other kinds of outside broadcasts, such as interviews or dramas, were recorded on film. Film equipment was smaller and lighter than normal studio equipment, but the film had to be processed before it could be broadcast.

These days even smaller, lighter portable video equipment is used instead. As the video tape does not need any processing it can be shown at once.

The centre of operations in an outside broadcast is the mobile control room. This is a large van which contains the equipment found in the production, sound and vision control rooms in a TV studio. All the pictures from the cameras are sent back here and the ones selected for broadcasting are then sent back to the TV station by radio waves or by cables.

Outside broadcasts

Most sports programmes and other events not staged specially for the TV cameras are outside broadcasts (usually referred to as "Oh bees") and parts of other programmes are made in this way too. The location need not be outdoors. OBs are often transmitted from theatres, concert halls and other indoor locations.

Commentators usually have a position overlooking the whole scene, but they also have TV monitors showing the pictures from each camera. They base their commentaries partly on what they can actually see and partly on the scenes on the monitors, so that they can fit their words to what the viewer can see.

Where land lines (cables) exist, signals are sent back to the TV station through them. If there are none available, the signals are sent by radio waves from a portable transmitting mast set up next to the van. The transmitting and receiving aerials are usually dish-shaped.

Production control area

Sound engineer

Vision engineer

Gun microphone

Camera 1

Camera and microphone cables plug in here.

News gathering

1

Speed is vitally important when gathering news stories. Video cameras can now be operated by one person, whereas the older video and film equipment needed two people, one for pictures and one for sound.

2

Broadcasting a live report from the scene of a news story is the fastest way of getting it on air. Vans like this have a small transmitter used to send the signal direct to the studio by microwave.

3

The less urgent news stories are recorded on video tape. They have to be rushed to the studio as quickly as possible. A motorbike messenger is usually the fastest way of getting it there.

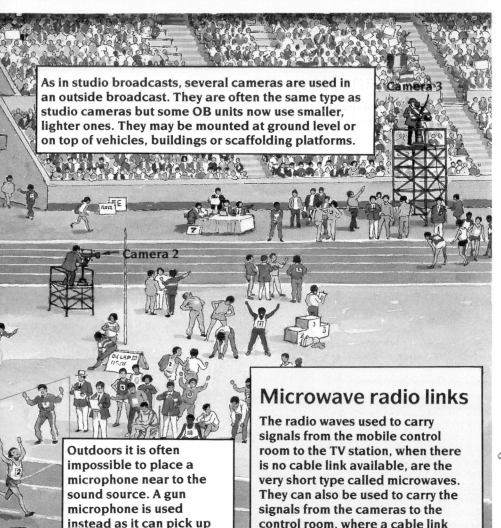

As in studio broadcasts, several cameras are used in an outside broadcast. They are often the same type as studio cameras but some OB units now use smaller, lighter ones. They may be mounted at ground level or on top of vehicles, buildings or scaffolding platforms.

Camera 3

Camera 2

Outdoors it is often impossible to place a microphone near to the sound source. A gun microphone is used instead as it can pick up sound from quite a distance away, coming from the direction in which it is pointed. A fluffy windshield is often fitted round the microphone to reduce noise caused by the wind.

Microwave radio links

The radio waves used to carry signals from the mobile control room to the TV station, when there is no cable link available, are the very short type called microwaves. They can also be used to carry the signals from the cameras to the control room, where a cable link would be too awkward.

Microwaves are used so that the signals do not interfere with radio signals being broadcast to people's homes. Microwaves cannot travel through objects so often have to be "bounced" to a series of aerials before reaching the TV station.

Filming on location

When programme makers use film cameras outside the studios, this is called filming on location. Many dramas contain filmed sequences. The location may not be outdoors. Often it is hard to make shots in a studio look realistic and it may be cheaper to use an existing building to get the right atmosphere and detail.

Clapperboard

Cameraman

Assistant cameraman

Sound recordist

PA

Director

Only one camera is used when filming on location, so each shot is carefully planned and prepared in advance. The sound is recorded separately on an ordinary sound tape recorder. A clapperboard is used at the beginning of each shot so that the sound and picture can be exactly matched (synchronized) when they are put together.

With a single camera, the same scene has to be repeated many times and filmed from different angles with various types of shots, such as close-ups and long shots. Later, the film editor has to choose the best performances and cut together the different shots to produce the most dramatic effect.

4

TV stations have special land lines and microwave links joining studios all over the country. So people being interviewed in one area, either in the studio or outside, can be seen and heard nationally.

5

Overseas links are made by communications satellites which carry telephone messages as well as TV signals. Mobile dish aerials like this make it possible to send live reports from almost anywhere.

In the control room

The control room is the place where a television programme is produced. The images from the cameras in the studio and pre-recorded film or video are combined with music, other soundtracks, graphics and titles ready for broadcasting. In a live programme, like the news broadcast shown here, this is all done as the programme is transmitted.

Recorded programmes are put on video tape to be shown at their scheduled time. The production team in the control room work with their colleagues on the studio floor to put the programme together. These pages show how it is done.

Who does what

The *producer* is in overall control of a programme and will have decided what it is about, its length and other editorial details. He or she is in charge of the whole team.

The *director* is responsible for what you see on the screen. He or she looks at the pictures from the cameras in the studio and on film or video and decides which should be broadcast and for how long. The director gives the studio staff instructions (known as "talkback") over their headphones.

The *vision mixer* follows the director's instructions to get each shot ready for transmission. He or she operates the controls of the vision mixing desk to get the appropriate effects, such as mixes or wipes (see page 16).

The *technical manager* is responsible for all the equipment in the studio and control room. He or she makes sure that everything is ready for the programme and that nothing goes wrong.

The *production assistant* (PA) checks the timing of shots and that everything is going to the producer's original plan.

The *floor manager* controls the action on the studio floor, following the director's instructions.

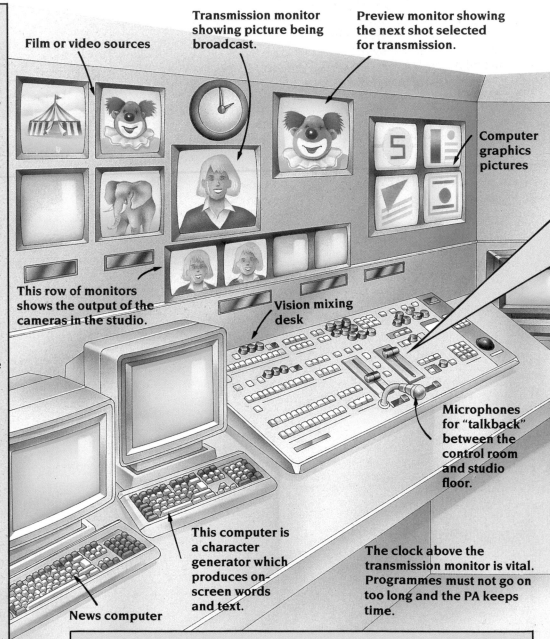

Film or video sources

Transmission monitor showing picture being broadcast.

Preview monitor showing the next shot selected for transmission.

Computer graphics pictures

This row of monitors shows the output of the cameras in the studio.

Vision mixing desk

Microphones for "talkback" between the control room and studio floor.

This computer is a character generator which produces on-screen words and text.

News computer

The clock above the transmission monitor is vital. Programmes must not go on too long and the PA keeps time.

On the screens

This picture shows control room equipment during a live news broadcast. The production team watch screens called monitors. Each picture source (studio and OB cameras, video tape, film and other studios) is shown on its own small monitor. The two larger monitors show the picture that is actually being broadcast (or recorded), and the next shot waiting to go out. They are called the transmission monitor and preview monitor. Yet more small monitors show the captions and other graphics, generated by special computers.

The vision mixing desk

The vision mixing desk is used to get shots ready for transmission and to mix and cut between them (see page 16 for more on this). The rows of buttons are known as buses, and the three lots of buses as banks.

In every bus there is one button for each camera, and for other picture sources, such as video tape and film. The vision mixer controls which picture is being transmitted, or recorded, by pressing the appropriate button. The buttons then light up to show which camera or source is being used.

The bottom two buses are the main bank, which is used for simple cuts between shots. More complex effects are set up in advance on the top two banks of buttons, and then passed on to the main bank.

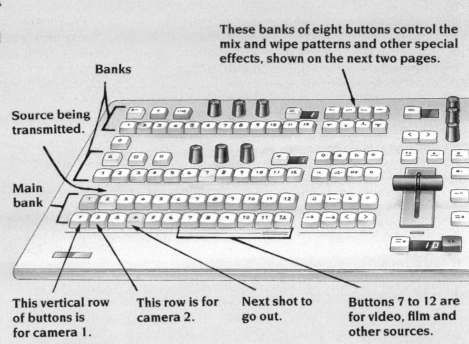

Banks

These banks of eight buttons control the mix and wipe patterns and other special effects, shown on the next two pages.

Source being transmitted.

Main bank

This vertical row of buttons is for camera 1.

This row is for camera 2.

Next shot to go out.

Buttons 7 to 12 are for video, film and other sources.

Reading the news

In the studio, the newsreader sits at a desk in front of the camera. There is a small computer built into the newsreader's desk to pass on updated information and instructions during the programme. She also wears an earpiece through which the director in the control room can speak to her during the broadcast, unheard by viewers. A small TV screen, unseen by the viewers at home, shows the newsreader the picture that is being transmitted.

A news programme usually needs only one or two cameras as the newsreader is sitting still, but there will be lots of video and film reports and live links with other studios and outside broadcasts too. The picture from these live links is often shown on a large TV screen next to the newsreader, so that she can see who she is speaking to and viewers can see both (see page 13).

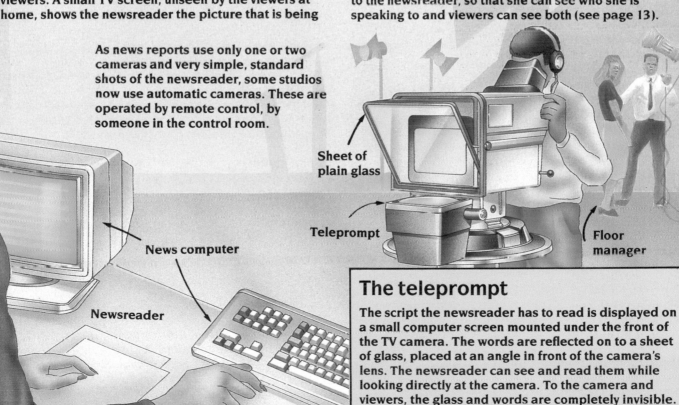

As news reports use only one or two cameras and very simple, standard shots of the newsreader, some studios now use automatic cameras. These are operated by remote control, by someone in the control room.

Sheet of plain glass

News computer

Teleprompt

Floor manager

Newsreader

The teleprompt

The script the newsreader has to read is displayed on a small computer screen mounted under the front of the TV camera. The words are reflected on to a sheet of glass, placed at an angle in front of the camera's lens. The newsreader can see and read them while looking directly at the camera. To the camera and viewers, the glass and words are completely invisible.

Special effects

The picture that appears on your TV screen is not always exactly like the live scene originally taken by the TV camera. In the control room or editing suite the image from one camera can be electronically combined with other images.

Combinations of different images in a single picture can create very magical or strange effects. Most of the time, however, we see them put to more ordinary uses in news programmes and the weather forecast for instance. These two pages, and pages 18-19, explain how some of the effects are created. See if you can spot them when watching TV.

Cuts, mixes and wipes

The most common and simple effects are ways of putting two different shots together. They are carried out by the vision mixer using the vision mixing desk shown on page 15. The pictures below show what simple cuts, mixes and wipes look like on screen.

Cuts are a straight change from one image to a different one.

Mixes gradually dissolve from one image to another, with the two combined as a single image in between.

Wipes look as if one picture is being peeled away to reveal another one underneath.

As digital, computer effects become more common, these simple effects are being used less often for some things. See pages 18-19 for more about the spectacular effects that computers can create.

Double shots

Here an actor (Fred One) appears on the screen, with himself (Fred Two). The two even have a conversation with each other. This is known as a double shot.

A double shot is achieved by shooting the same scene twice. First Fred One keeps to the left of the set and is careful to leave pauses long enough for Fred Two's replies when speaking. This scene is recorded on video tape A. Then the actor becomes Fred Two. Now he keeps only to the right of the set and leaves pauses for Fred One's conversation, which has already been recorded. As the camera does not move between shots, it ensures that the background matches exactly in both shots.

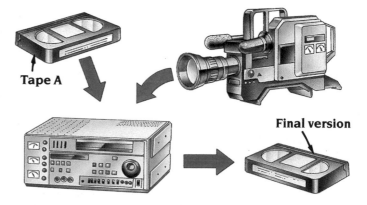

Tape A

Final version

The signal from tape A is sent to the vision mixing desk at the same time as the shot of Fred Two. The two signals are combined and recorded on a new video tape. The final version shows two identical Freds having a talk.

Chromakey

Chromakey is the most common technique used for combining two images. It can be used to create fantastical effects and images which would be impossible to shoot in the ordinary way. Chromakey works by removing all parts of a picture that are in one "key" colour. A bright blue is usually chosen, as skin does not contain much blue.

The newsreader sits in front of a bright blue background. The camera's output is passed through a processor which removes all the blue to produce a "key signal", which is the image of the newsreader only. This key signal then goes through an electronic switch. This fills in the empty background, where the blue used to be, with images from another source. A combined or "composite" picture is created.

Here, a weather map is being shot by camera 2. However, the new background can come from any source: film, video, other cameras, or even an outside broadcast.

Chromakey effects

This is a how a flying carpet scene would be created. The background shows a moving sky filmed from a plane.

Chromakey can also be used to distort the scale of things in a scene. To achieve this effect the cat is shot close up, and the man from a distance.

The switch can be altered to let through only the key colour, instead of rejecting it. This makes the foreground image disappear, leaving an empty shape to be filled by the other source. Here is a dancing figure of flames, created by combining shots of a dancer with video of a fire.

Using the double shot technique described on the left, together with chromakey for the little figure, allows a tiny Fred Two to dance on his own giant Fred One hand. Fred One is prerecorded and Fred Two shot from a distance.

To make someone vanish into thin air, a figure is first chromakeyed into a landscape. Then the vision mixer mixes from the composite shot to the background alone. This makes the figure slowly fade and disappear.

Digital effects

The kinds of special effects shown on the previous two pages are all done using the ordinary vision mixing desk. Although impressive, they are just ways of combining different shots. For really spectacular effects a computer is required.

A digital effects computer manipulates the images from a TV camera or on video or film in different ways. Pictures can be re-coloured, combined with elements of other pictures, images squeezed, squashed and stretched, twisted, tilted and turned, moved around the screen, repeated, mirrored and split. Some of these digital effects are shown below.

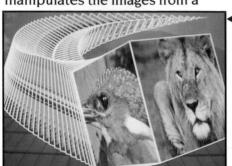

◄ Moving TV pictures, even live action, appear in the four faces of this spinning cube.

◄ A moving picture splits into four sliding slices.

A mosaic patch, ▲ often used to conceal a face.

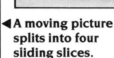

◄ Moving pictures are shown on these intersecting planes, against any background.

▲ This effect is called solarization.

Picture magic

This sequence of photographs shows how real images can be combined with computer created graphics, for incredible effects.

1　　2　　3

How a digital effects computer works

Like all computers, TV effects machines are digital machines, and handle information as a series of separate pulses. The signal from a TV camera, however, is not digital, but a continuous, constantly varying current of electricity. This kind of information is known as "analogue" information.

3 The digitized picture signal is sent to a part of the computer called the frame store. This holds the information for one complete TV picture at a time so that it can be worked on.

5 Digital effects machines are quite slow as they work frame by frame, and it takes 30 or 25 frames to make one second of TV (see page 25). It also takes a great deal of memory to hold all of this picture

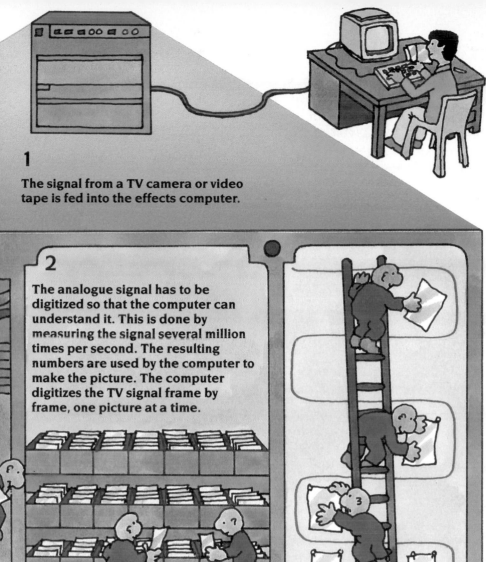

1

The signal from a TV camera or video tape is fed into the effects computer.

2

The analogue signal has to be digitized so that the computer can understand it. This is done by measuring the signal several million times per second. The resulting numbers are used by the computer to make the picture. The computer digitizes the TV signal frame by frame, one picture at a time.

3

4

While the image is in the frame store the designer manipulates it, for example changing some colours or shapes, combining images or even drawing on top.

information. So these computers are used mostly for creating still pictures, such as backgrounds for text, maps or photos or for short moving sequences such as adverts and titles.

6 The final image has to be reconverted to an analogue signal to be broadcast. Some TV cameras produce digital output which can be used directly by computers. Engineers are working to produce digital broadcasts and TV sets.

Digital painting

Colour palette

Mouse

Graphics tablet

Keyboard

Certain kinds of computers can generate TV Images from scratch. These graphics computers, sometimes called TV "paintboxes", produce video output. Designers or artists use an electronic pen or mouse with the graphics tablet to create a picture, which is displayed on the screen. They can produce images in any style, from pencil drawings to watercolour paintings. The computer can also "grab" a video image for the designer to manipulate.

Video libraries

The tiny disk holds thousands of photos.

Still TV pictures can also be stored on computer in video libraries. These often use laser disks, rather like music CDs, or even memory chips. Each picture is named and can be called up very fast, as computers can read any part of the disk or memory instantly, instead of having to go backwards and forwards as with a tape. Picture libraries are used to store things like photographs of the world's famous politicians, pop and film stars or athletes.

Recording and editing

Most programmes are recorded and edited before being broadcast. Even live, unedited programmes are recorded so that there is a permanent record.

Editing is the process of assembling a series of different scenes or shots into a continuous programme, of the right length. With programmes made up of scenes shot and recorded "as live" (that is, the vision mixed output of several cameras), there may be mistakes to cut too. Editing is even more vital to programmes like dramas, shot on film with a single camera, and documentaries, where editing involves getting the structure right, selecting material and reshuffling it to tell the story in the best way.

How tape recording works

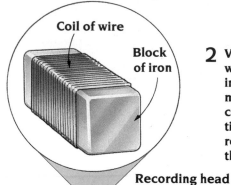

Coil of wire

Block of iron

Recording head

1 The electric signal from the studio or TV camera is sent to a recording head, which is an electromagnet made up of a coil of wire wrapped around a tiny block of iron. When the signal goes through the wire, the iron block becomes magnetized. Its magnetic strength varies with the strength of the electric signal.

2 Video tape is made of plastic, coated with a thin layer of tiny particles of iron oxide. This layer becomes magnetized as the tape comes into contact with the recording head. The tiny particles form into a pattern in response to the magnetic strength of the block of iron.

Iron oxide particles in random pattern before recording.

Blank tape

3 When the tape is rewound and played back, it passes over the recording head again. This time the head works in reverse and converts the magnetic pattern into an electrical signal. This signal is sent to the TV set and seen as pictures on the screen.

Recorded tape

Iron oxide particles form a regular pattern once recorded.

Moving heads

In sound recording, the sound is recorded in straight lines along the tape. For video recording a way had to be found to pack a greater volume of information on to a tape. If the sound recording system was used it would take 100km (62 miles) of tape to record a one hour programme, instead of the 150m (165yd) needed with the video system.

To overcome this problem the recording heads on a video tape recorder (VTR) also move as the tape moves past them. They lay the information as diagonal tracks across the tape. This fits more information into the space. Each diagonal track is the information for half of one single still "frame" or TV picture.*

The sound signal for the TV programme is recorded by a separate sound recording head and laid down as a straight track along the edge of the tape.

The tape moves at about 100mm (4in) per second.

The spinning of the heads makes the speed of recording even faster — about 6m (6.5yd) or more per second.

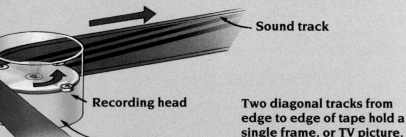

Sound track

Recording head

Drum

Two diagonal tracks from edge to edge of tape hold a single frame, or TV picture.

There are several recording heads mounted on a wheel inside a drum. Some systems use four heads, as shown here, others just two. The tape wraps around the drum in a spiral path, and as it does so, the wheel and heads spin in the opposite direction.

To make later editing easier, each frame on a video has an identifying number, called a timecode. This is recorded on the tape as an electronic code, at the same time as the sound and the pictures. Some home video recorders and cameras have this facility too. Domestic video recorders work in exactly the same way as the broadcast VTRs shown here.

*For more about how we see still TV pictures as moving, look on pages 24 and 25.

Video editing

Video tape editing is done by copying material from one tape to another. This is called "dubbing" and needs at least two machines. The source VTR plays the first tape with the scenes required, and the master VTR records these selected pieces, with invisible joins, on to a master tape. Several VTRs are used so that it is possible to mix from one source to another, using a vision mixing desk.

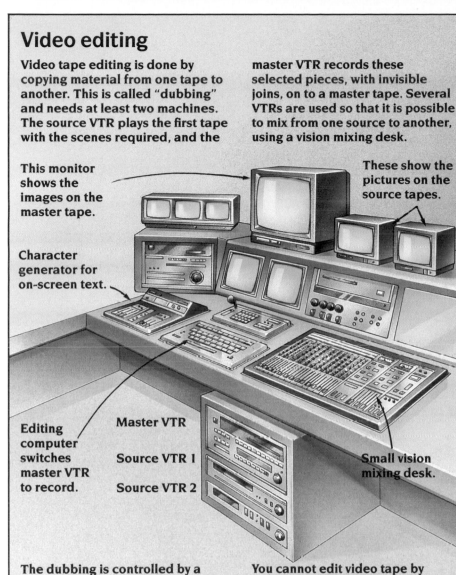

This monitor shows the images on the master tape.

Character generator for on-screen text.

These show the pictures on the source tapes.

Editing computer switches master VTR to record.

Master VTR

Source VTR 1

Source VTR 2

Small vision mixing desk.

The dubbing is controlled by a special computer, using the timecodes recorded on the video tapes. It is programmed to switch the master VTR from play to record when the tape in the source machine reaches the timecode of the chosen shot.

You cannot edit video tape by cutting it and joining the pieces together. This is partly because you cannot see the images on the tape so it would be very hard to know where to cut. Cuts cause picture disturbance and joins can damage the recording heads.

Film editing

In film editing you can actually see the picture on each frame and can cut and join it. The original negatives are processed by a laboratory and "work" or "rush" prints made. The editor cuts these and joins selected pieces together with transparent tape. Next, the original negative is cut and joined up, using a chemical "cement", to match the work print. A final "show print" with no joins is then made, by sandwiching together the edited negative with unexposed film and shining a light through them.

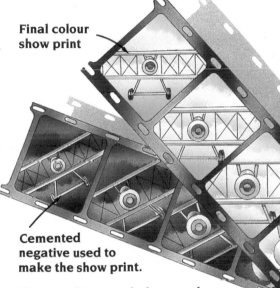

Final colour show print

Cemented negative used to make the show print.

The sound is recorded on another film coated with magnetic particles, like sound tape. On the editing bench the sprocket holes keep the picture and sound films locked together so that the editor can cut and join both at once and keep pictures and sound synchronized.

Editing at home

If you have a video camera and a video cassette recorder (VCR), you can edit the tapes that you make. The camera acts as the source, and the VCR makes the master tape.

First view your tape on the TV screen to decide which sections you want to use, and in what order. Then view the tape through the camera's viewfinder and use the tape counter to list where these shots are on the tape.

Connect the camera to the VCR's input socket so that it will record from the camera. Then using the camera's viewfinder to view the source tape, record your shots in the new sequence. Run the tape backwards and forwards to get to the scenes you want, leaving out any material that you don't want. Most cameras and VCRs have dubbing and editing features to help you get the joins between scenes as invisible as possible. Many can even do simple vision mixing, add a new sound track and even on-screen text.

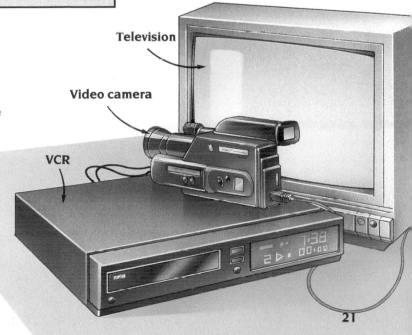

Television

Video camera

VCR

Transmitting TV pictures

Most people receive the pictures on their TV sets through the air. Electronic signals from the TV station are sent along cables to a transmitting station. There they are combined with radio waves and sent out via the air. Aerials connected to TV sets in people's homes pick up these signals.

Sometimes underground cables are used to carry the signals. This method is used in places where there are problems involved in transmitting signals through the air. Satellites are used to transmit programmes over very long distances. Both cable and satellite systems can be used for "pay-TV", where viewers pay the broadcasting company.

Radio waves go out in all directions, rather like light from a lighthouse.

In the transmitter

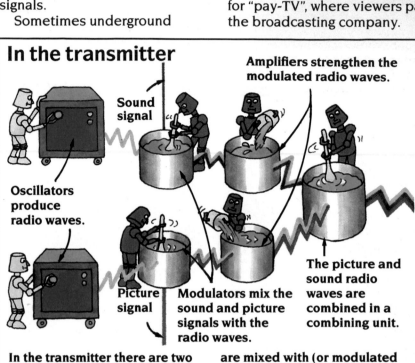

Amplifiers strengthen the modulated radio waves.

Sound signal

Oscillators produce radio waves.

Picture signal

Modulators mix the sound and picture signals with the radio waves.

The picture and sound radio waves are combined in a combining unit.

In the transmitter there are two "oscillators". These make two radio waves, one to carry the picture information and one to carry the sound information. The two radio waves are sent to two "modulators" where they are mixed with (or modulated by) the sound and vision signals. The modulated radio waves are then amplified (strengthened by amplifiers), combined together and fed to the transmitting aerials.

The transmitting aerial sends out the radio waves in all directions. The type of radio waves used to carry signals are made very much weaker if they travel through solid objects, so transmitting aerials are usually positioned high up, so that the signals do not hit any obstructions.

The receiving aerial picks up the signals and sends them down a cable to the TV set.

Radio waves

Long wave (low frequency)

Short wave (high frequency)

Radio waves are described either by their wavelength (the distance between the top of one wave and the top of the next) or by their frequency (the number of waves per second). Long waves have low frequencies, short waves have high frequencies. TV signals are usually transmitted on very high frequency (VHF) waves, or ultra high frequency (UHF) waves.

All TV companies broadcasting in a single area must use different wavelengths to transmit their signals. If they used the same one, or ones that were too close, the signals would get jumbled up and impossible for TV sets to sort out.

Transmitting by radio waves

Radio waves from TV transmitters cannot travel much more than about 80km (50 miles). To broadcast over larger distances, TV companies need several transmitters to pick up the signal from each other and pass it on in turn. Where there are mountains which would obstruct the signal, it must be carried over, either by a transmitter at the top or by land line.

People living near mountains sometimes receive the same signal twice – once direct from the transmitter and once after it has bounced off the mountain and back to the aerial. The result is called "ghosting", a faint shadow picture to the side of the main picture. To avoid this problem a local relay station is sometimes built. It picks up the main signal and rebroadcasts it on a different wavelength. People having difficulty receiving the main signal can tune their sets to this frequency.

Satellite transmissions

The best way of broadcasting over very large distances is to use a satellite. TV satellites orbit over the Equator, 35,786km (22,237 miles) high. At this height and position they take exactly 24 hours to orbit Earth, and so always stay above the same bit of the Earth, which turns at the same speed. This is known as a "geostationary" orbit. The area that a satellite broadcasts to is called its "footprint".

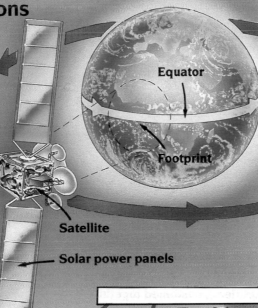

Equator

Footprint

Satellite

Solar power panels

Earth station

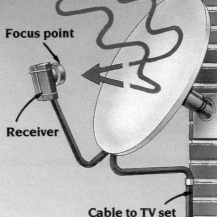

Focus point

Receiver

Cable to TV set

The TV signal is transmitted into space by a large dish aerial, known as an earth station. The satellite picks up the signal, amplifies it and sends it back to Earth. In order to receive satellite signals, you need a small dish aerial, pointing exactly to the satellite's position in the sky. The dish focuses the TV signal (rather as a lens focuses light) into a receiver connected to the TV set.

Transmitting by cable

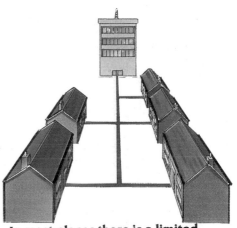

In most places there is a limited number of radio frequencies that TV stations can use for broadcasting. However, in some areas, TV signals can also be sent out down networks of underground cables.

Glass fibre optic cable

Plastic casing

The latest systems can carry dozens of channels at a time. They use fibre optic cables which are made from ultra fine threads of glass, as thin as hair. The signal is carried by pulses of laser light.

How TV sets work

The job of a TV set is to turn the electronic signals created by TV cameras and microphones back into pictures and sound. The TV's aerial picks up the signals from the transmitting aerials and they then travel down a cable to the aerial socket at the back of the TV.

When you switch on the set, the sound and picture signals are separated from each other and from the carrier waves. The sound is sent to the TV's loudspeaker. The picture signal is sent to the picture tube, which converts it into the pictures that you watch on the screen.

How the picture tube works

1. When the picture signal has been separated from the sound signal, it is split into its three separate colour signals – red, blue and green. The TV's picture tube converts these electric signals back into light on the screen. The type of tube shown here is called a shadow mask tube. There are other kinds but this is the most common.

2. At the back of the picture tube there are three electron guns that fire beams of electrons at the screen. Electrons are parts of atoms. All atoms have a nucleus in the middle with electrons spinning round it. The electrons carry an electric charge. The amount of electricity leaving each gun is controlled by the strength of the original signal.

3. The screen is the front of the picture tube. It is covered with tiny stripes or dots of a chemical called phosphor. Three different types of phosphor are used. One glows red when hit by electrons, one glows green and one glows blue.

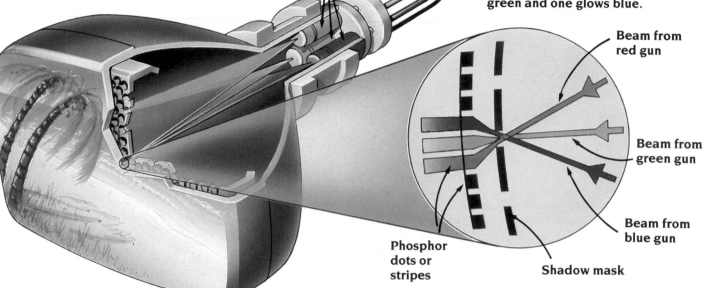

Electron guns

Beam from red gun

Beam from green gun

Beam from blue gun

Shadow mask

Phosphor dots or stripes

4. A strong electron beam makes the phosphor glow brightly and a weak beam makes it glow dimly. The beams are directed at each of the sets of three phosphor dots or stripes one at a time, starting at the top left hand corner and working across and down the screen.

5. Behind the screen is a metal plate with thousands of tiny holes in it, called a shadow mask There is one hole for every three dots of phosphor on the screen. The mask is positioned so that each of the three electron beams can strike only the right type of phosphor: red beam on red phosphor and so on.

Moving pictures

Although a TV looks as if it is showing moving pictures it is in fact a series of still frames, shown in quick succession. Any picture the brain receives takes one tenth of a second to fade away. This is known as "persistence of vision". TV stations broadcast 24 or 25 frames per second, so you see them as continuous, life-like movement.

Cinema film, like that shown here, works in a similar way and is shown at a speed of 24 frames per second. You can actually see the individual still images when you look at a strip of film like this. Each frame on the film strip is very slightly different from its neighbours.

Tricking the eyes

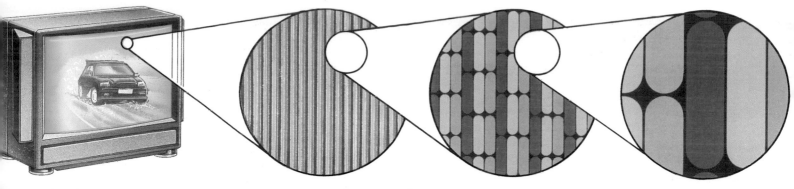

If you look very closely at a TV screen you can see that the picture is made up of lots of horizontal lines. There are 625 lines in Europe and much of the rest of the world, and 525 in America and Japan. These lines are made up of the tiny dots or stripes of phosphor, which glow red, blue or green in response to the broadcast signal. Most screens have over a million of these dots. The three colours mix in your eyes to produce all the realistic colours you see on

the screen.

The picture is actually created just one dot at a time. Each dot lights up and fades in turn along each line, line by line down the screen. This happens so fast that every dot on the screen seems to be lit up all of the time and so you see a complete picture. This is another example of the "persistence of vision" effect which makes us see moving pictures, described on the previous page.

Selecting a channel

TV sets offer a choice of programmes from the various broadcasting stations. The radio waves that carry the TV signals are divided into channels according to their wavelength and frequency.* Within each area, each station is given a different channel, so that they will be using different frequencies to transmit their signals. There are gaps between channels to make sure that they do not interfere with each other.

When the radio waves enter the TV set they pass into a tuner. The tuner will only allow waves within a certain band of frequencies to pass on to be shown on the screen. It is adjustable so that it will let any single band through. You can adjust, or "tune" the TV set to let through the channel you want to watch. When you first get a new TV set you may have to tune it to local frequencies. Any button can be preset to any station.

Remote controls

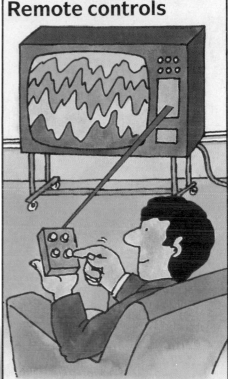

Most TV sets have remote controls for changing channels and operating the volume and other controls. They work by sending the TV set instructions by means of an infra-red light beam. This carries the instructions in a light code, similar to morse code. A sensor inside the TV set picks up the infra-red light and translates it into electrical signals. A decoder then sends this information to the right place in the TV set.

The tuner is adjusted to let through the waves for the channel you select.

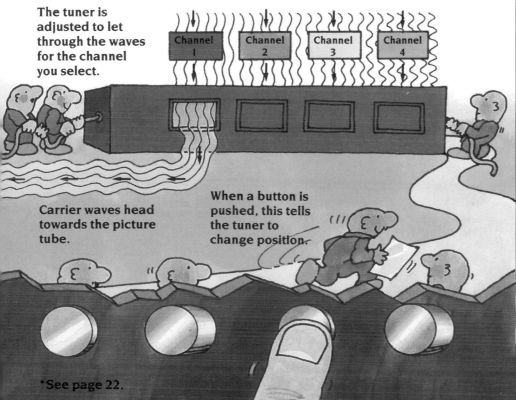

Channel 1 Channel 2 Channel 3 Channel 4

Carrier waves head towards the picture tube.

When a button is pushed, this tells the tuner to change position.

*See page 22.

Teletext

Teletext is an on-screen information service, broadcast by some TV stations. The screens of text and graphics are known as "pages". They are broadcast at the same time as ordinary programmes, but you need a special receiver in your TV to be able to display them. Special keys on the remote control handset enable you to tell the TV to show the pages that you want to see.

The sort of information broadcast includes news headlines, weather forecasts, TV listings, information from TV programmes such as recipes, and even viewer's jokes and pictures.

Instant information

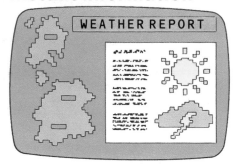

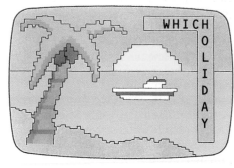

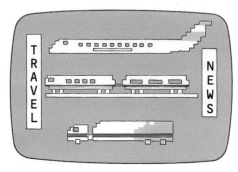

Teletext pages are put together on computer at the TV station, using text, together with small blocks of colour to form simple pictures, like those shown here. The big advantage of teletext is that it is very easy and quick to update. This makes it very useful for information which is constantly changing, such as news and financial prices. Teletext is often used for extra information as a back-up to TV programmes, but you can also use it to check information difficult to find elsewhere, such as details of roadworks.

Datacasts

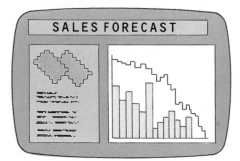

Datacasts are special teletext pages, only available to people who pay for the service. The information is sent out scrambled so that it cannot be viewed by non-subscribers.

Subtitles

Subtitles for the deaf are broadcast as teletext at the same time as some programmes. The ordinary TV picture fills most of the screen and the subtitle goes in a little box.

How teletext works

The pages are made up and stored on computer as digital signals. These are then broadcast in the same way as ordinary programme signals. At the top of each TV screen there are some spare lines which are not normally used for the TV picture, and these are used to carry the teletext signals. If your TV is wrongly adjusted, you may be able to see them as flashes of white light at the top of the screen. There are also spare lines used to carry information for TV engineers.

Digital teletext signals   Spare lines

Receiving teletext

All the teletext pages are numbered and they are broadcast in sequence. When you choose a page, the TV set waits until this one is transmitted, which may be 20 seconds or so, and then displays it. This page is stored and displayed by your TV until you choose another page or switch the TV set off.

The most popular pages, such as TV programme listings, the weather forecast or stockmarket prices appear more than once in the sequence to reduce the waiting time.

TV games and computers

An ordinary TV set can be used as a display screen for home computers and computer games. Business computers have their own special display screens called monitors, which cannot get TV broadcasts. Ordinary TVs are fine for showing video games, but not as good for more serious computer applications such as word processing as they do not give such a detailed picture as a proper computer monitor.

Our use of television is being revolutionized by compact laser disks which can be played and viewed in a completely new way, as described here.

Video games and home computers

A TV, or video, games system consists of a console, which is capable of playing several different games, but cannot carry out other computer functions such as word processing. Unlike a computer, the console does not have a keyboard, but a pair of joysticks, or other controllers, to control the on-screen action.

Home computers can also play games programs, although these are often not so high in graphics quality as video games. A computer can do many other things too and so is more versatile. The computer's keyboard has special function keys as well as ordinary letter and number keys, but can use joysticks too.

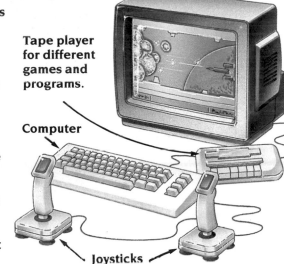

Tape player for different games and programs.

Computer

Joysticks

CD-TV

The small compact discs (like music CDs) used by TV stations to store still images in picture libraries, can also record moving video images, and this is known as CD-TV. It is very good for commercial applications such as education and for presenting information in places like shops and museums. There are home discs and players too.

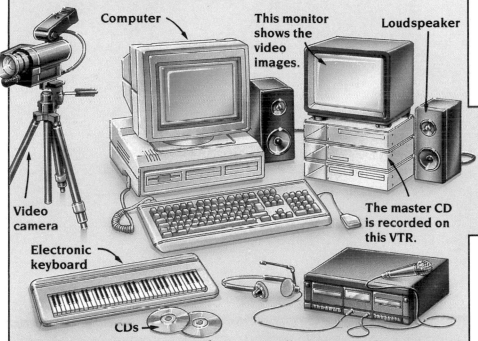

Computer

This monitor shows the video images.

Loudspeaker

Video camera

Electronic keyboard

CDs

The master CD is recorded on this VTR.

A CD-TV programme is put together using a computer and special software. It can include ordinary moving video, still shots, computer graphics, music, voice-overs and on-screen text.

The advantage of the CD is that you do not have to start at the beginning and fast-forward or rewind to find the bit you want. You can call up any part of a programme in the same way as on a music CD, and this is known as "random access". This means that you can view the TV in a new way. Instead of watching a programme from start to finish you can interact with it, first choosing what interests you most, repeating things, skipping bits and dipping in at random, instantly.

Interactive video

The CD-TV disc needs a special player, which allows you to interact with the programme on the disc. A player includes a remote control handset which you use to move a pointer round the screen. You point the pointer at things on screen to choose options from on-screen text menus, return to the menu, go back or forwards and so on. Many screens also have areas you can point at to get more information.

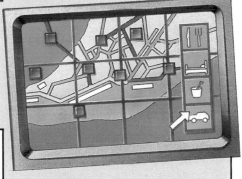

For example, if you point at the red "graphic buttons" on this on-screen map, the screen changes and gives you information about what is there. You can also ask to see where all the beaches, car parks, hotels or restaurants are, by pointing at the pictures, or "icons" down the side. There is also a video presentation about the town and a text diary of events. This sort of CD-TV is used in tourist information centres.

Home video equipment

The development of small, inexpensive electronic cameras and recorders easy enough for people to use at home, is causing a revolution in home entertainment.

At the centre of the video revolution is the video cassette recorder (VCR), which gives a far greater choice of viewing than is possible with a TV set alone.

Home video cameras are less common, but becoming more widespread as they get cheaper, more sophisticated and easier to use. They can be rented for special occasions, like holidays and weddings, and many schools and colleges have one.

Video cassette recorders

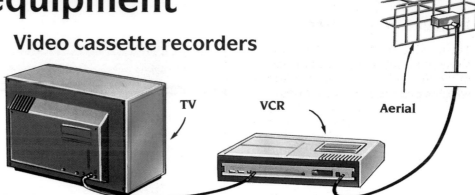

TV   VCR   Aerial

A VCR is the domestic version of the video tape recorder used in TV broadcasting. The VCR picks up broadcast signals directly from the TV aerial. A lead from the aerial plugs into the aerial socket at the back of the VCR. Another lead connects the VCR to the TV set. To record a programme the signal is transferred to the tape via the recording heads of the VCR. To watch programmes on the TV as they are broadcast, the signal comes from the aerial, through the VCR to the TV set.

VCR features

With a VCR you can choose when to watch TV programmes, rather than having to do so only when they are broadcast. Also, once you have taped a programme you can watch it as often as you like. Taping broadcast programmes to watch later is known as "timeshift".

Cinema films, cartoons, TV programmes and specialist subjects such as exercise routines are also available on video tape, to buy or to rent, so you can watch them in the comfort of your own home.

A VCR has its own tuner, so it acts quite independently of the TV. This means you can watch the same programme as you are recording, or a different channel, or it can record when the TV is turned off.

VCRs have a timer so that you can set it in advance to record a particular programme whilst you are out.

Most VCRs have special facilities which let you watch a video in a way impossible with an ordinary broadcast programme. For example, you can pause a tape and look at a single still frame. You can also view a video tape frame by frame, or in slow motion, fast forward and even going backwards. Some VCR machines have variable speeds for these functions, others are pre-set.

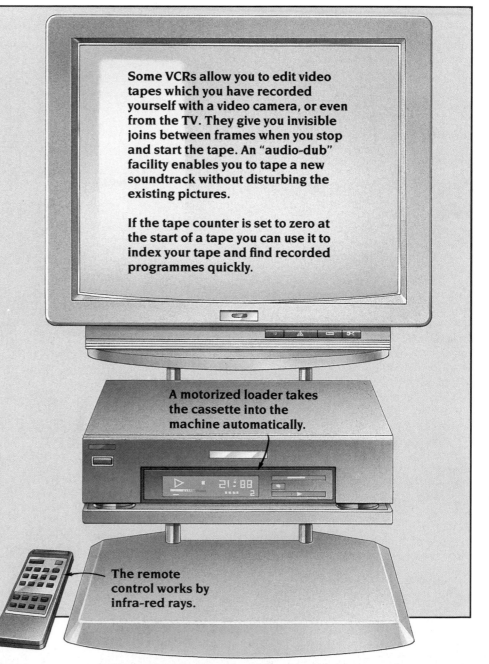

Some VCRs allow you to edit video tapes which you have recorded yourself with a video camera, or even from the TV. They give you invisible joins between frames when you stop and start the tape. An "audio-dub" facility enables you to tape a new soundtrack without disturbing the existing pictures.

If the tape counter is set to zero at the start of a tape you can use it to index your tape and find recorded programmes quickly.

A motorized loader takes the cassette into the machine automatically.

The remote control works by infra-red rays.

Picture in picture

The most sophisticated VCRs can show you what is being broadcast on other channels while you are already watching one channel or a video. They can also show a video while you are watching broadcast programmes.

The main picture fills most of the screen. A small area within it displays another whole screen, but reduced in size, which shows what is on the video or another channel. This facility is often known as "picture in picture" or PIP.

Screen display

Many VCRs can also show on-screen messages. These may tell you what channel you are watching, the date and time, show a list of programmes you want it to record and visual displays for sound volume, colour and other TV controls.

VCR television

Developments in electronics, and the possibility of smaller tapes, mean that TV sets and VCRs can be combined into one integrated machine. They still need two tuners in order to do all the things shown on these pages.

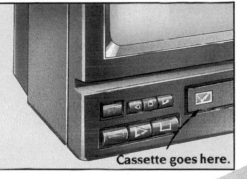

Cassette goes here.

Bar code programmer

Some VCRs can be set to record a program using bar codes – black and white lines like those to be found on most products in shops. Each channel, day of the week and time of day has its own bar code. The bar codes are read by a tiny laser beam in a handset, which is wiped over them.

The handset then sends this information about the programme you want to record to the VCR by infra-red rays. The VCR comes with a sheet printed with bar codes for each day, time and channel. Some TV listings magazines print the day and time bar codes for each programme.

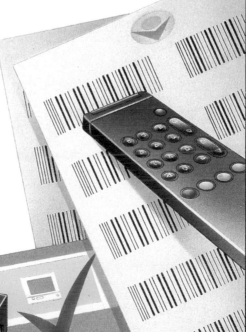

Video cameras

Home video cameras are sometimes known as "camcorders", a combination of the names camera and recorder. This is because the first home video cameras were rather like TV cameras, as they did not contain a video tape, but had to be connected to a VCR in order to record. These days cameras are more sophisticated and contain the tape and recording mechanism. Most use smaller format tapes than those used in VCRs.

As with VCRs, more expensive and newer machines have more features, such as stereo sound, still or slow frame recording, automatic fading and editing controls.

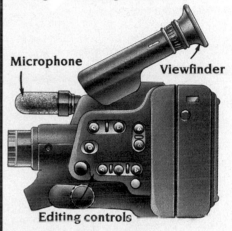

Microphone

Viewfinder

Editing controls

All cameras have a built-in microphone and automatically record sounds as well as pictures. However, you can change the soundtrack later if you want, using the audio-dub on a VCR, or even on the camera itself.

The viewfinder which you look through is not a glass lens, as on an ordinary stills camera, but a mini electronic screen, as on a full size TV camera. It shows exactly what the camera is recording.

Video cameras usually focus automatically on the main object in the viewfinder. The motorized zoom allows you to move smoothly between close-ups, mid-shots and long-shots.

Using a video camera

When using a video camera, you need to be aware of the same factors as if you were using a stills camera: focusing, the amount of light, and careful positioning of your subject. You also need to think about a few things that apply to taking moving pictures. The advantage of video is that you can experiment as much as you like, as tape can be rerecorded over and over again.

◄ It is important to keep the camera steady while you are shooting. Sequences that jump and jerk about are very difficult to watch. It is often a good idea to rest your camera on a firm surface. Better still, use a tripod so that you can turn the camera and tip it up and down while shooting. Some cameras are designed to be hand-held, others to rest on your shoulder. When holding and moving with the camera, try to move your whole body as smoothly as possible.

Camera shots

Any programme is composed of a series of separate shots. A shot is one individual scene. Each time you stop the camera, it is the end of the shot. It is a good idea to vary your shots to provide visual interest, taking your subject from several different angles and distances.

You get the best results from planning your shots in advance and thinking about how one shot will lead into another. Try to make each shot at least ten seconds long. If they are any shorter the result will be rather jumpy and fragmented. Never move the camera too quickly as fast movements look confusing on screen. Here are some of the most basic shots to try out and combine.

A long shot gives the general setting without much detail. It is useful for introducing viewers to a subject and for endings.

Panning is turning the camera from side to side during a shot. Move the camera slowly, otherwise shots seem confused. A pan of 360° should take at least one minute, so count in seconds as you shoot.

In a mid shot the main subject and background have equal importance.

Another way of varying shots is to change the height from which you shoot. The tendency is to shoot from one height – yours or a tripod's. Try lying on the floor and shooting upwards, or standing on something.

Tilting is tipping the camera up or down. It is a good idea to hold the camera still for about three seconds before starting to tilt, or pan, and when completing shots.

Close-ups have most impact on the viewer. All the attention is on the main subject and the background becomes unimportant. Remember to leave a border area.

With a zoom lens you can move between long shots and close-ups without moving the camera closer. Move the zoom slowly and smoothly, fast zoom can be disturbing.

TV development

Television technology has developed a great deal since its first introduction in the late 1930s. All sorts of astonishing innovations have taken place and more are in the pipeline.

There already are tiny TVs; in the future there may be TVs on a wrist watch and VCRs the size of personal stereos that you can view on the move. Tiny compact video disks (CVDs) may take the place of conventional video tapes. This page shows some of the more unusual kinds of TV already developed.

Huge TV

Giant screens are used at large-scale pop concerts and other events to show the action on stage. The huge screen works on the same principle as an ordinary TV set, but is made up of many small TV sets, each showing one colour, red, blue or green – like the phosphor dots of an ordinary TV set. From a distance it appears as a big picture.

Stage

Giant screen shows close-up of singer.

Multi-screens

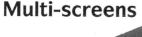

Screens showing same image, large and small.

This "video wall" is a popular effect on TV shows and is also used for advertising and promotion, rather like a "video poster". The bank of TV screens can all show the same, normal-size image, or each screen can be fed just part of the signal so that together they display a giant picture, or even a complex mix of images, as shown here.

HDTV

Large screen HDTV

Screen sizes have become larger, but, as the picture gets bigger, the detail decreases. Increasing the number of lines per frame overcomes this problem and is known as high-definition television (HDTV). HDTV has over a thousand lines per frame, but needs special cameras, TV sets, VCRs and even new ways of transmitting signals.

Mini TVs

Many manufacturers are producing tiny, battery-operated, truly portable TVs – the TV equivalent of the personal stereo. As it is difficult to miniaturize conventional screen technology enough, mini TVs mostly have a liquid crystal display screen, similar to those used in calculators or portable computers.

Digital TV sets

Some TV sets can store several still frames as digital information. This means that you can view several channels at once, as still pictures, or watch a broadcast as a sequence of small, still freeze frames, like those shown here. You can also store any screen image to view at a later stage.

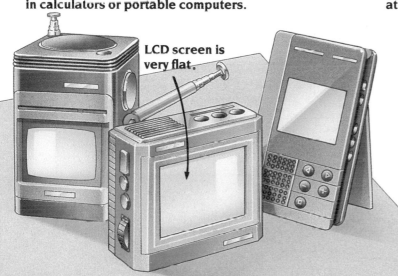

LCD screen is very flat.

The TV screen is split into 9 or 16 still pictures to show a freeze frame sequence.

Index

The publishers would like to thank Quantel UK and Questech Ltd for their kind permission to use the photographs on page 18.

This edition first published in 1992 by Usborne Publishing Ltd, Usborne House, 83-85 Saffron Hill, London EC1N 8RT.